"Baxter draws you along a knife's edge of tension from the first page to the last, leaving your heart thumping and sweat on your brow."
– *Midwest Book Review*

GOLDEN FORTUNE, DRAGON JADE

Alan Baxter

GOLDEN FORTUNE, DRAGON JADE

First Trade Paperback Edition - March 2020
Copyright © 2016 Alan Baxter
Cover Design © 2020 Alan Baxter
Internal layout by David Wood

Alan Baxter
www.alanbaxter.com.au

ISBN: 978-0-9805782-7-0

For Chen, Yong Fa
My Sifu

FOREWORD

I'd always wanted to write something in the vein of the great wuxia (martial heroes) kung fu epics I've loved so much my whole life. I've been a career martial artist for almost four decades, so kung fu has been an integral part of me for pretty much forever. But I'm a horror and dark fantasy writer for the most part, and had never got around finding a good story to scratch that wuxia itch. Then, back in 2016, Lindy Cameron of *Clan Destine Press* asked me to write a story for her new anthology. She wanted big stories, full of epic adventure, with fantasy or science fiction cores. But the story also needed to be a bit more family-friendly than my usual fare. And it needed an Australian connection. This is what came of that request.

The two protagonists in this yarn are cousins – he a Shaolin monk, her an accomplished geomancer. The Shaolin monk, Yong Fa, shares his first name with my Sifu, my kung fu teacher, in a subtle homage to him, and the character shows some of my teacher's irreverence and cheekiness, but is otherwise an entirely made up person. The character certainly isn't based on my Sifu. The geomancer, Zi Yi, is altogether more serious and focussed, but an accomplished mage in her own right. Together their skills are complementary and that's just as well when they realise the scale of their task, the distance they have to go to track down their missing jade dragon, and the kind of unforgiving country they'll be led to.

I'd had a nebulous idea for this Chinese-inspired fantasy story in mind for ages, with Shaolin martial arts and spirit magic, travel and adventure, but never quite had the framework to make it sing. Then the request for the story from *Clan Destine Press* said it needed an Australian connection of some kind, and I realised that setting this Chinese fantasy towards end of the Aussie gold rush would be perfect. It made the original idea better, and I was able to give a historical nod to my adopted country. It all catalysed into what I hope is an exciting novella.

You should check out the two volumes of **And Then..?** from *Clan Destine Press*, but as this is a story that's unlikely to ever find its way into one of my collections, I thought it would be a good idea to release it on its own as a chapbook. And as I have more room to spare now, this is a slightly expanded and embellished version compared to the one originally published. I got to add a few flourishes I had to cut out before.

It was a hell of a lot of fun to write, and I hope people have at least as much fun reading it.

Alan Baxter, NSW, 2020

1

Near Jiangmen, southern China, April 1859

Li Yong Fa paused among pine trees on the ridge and gazed into the valley below. Nestled in a deep vee of pale grey rock, bisected by a clear, rushing stream, was Long-en, the village of his birth. The houses with their red and green roof tiles and tan burnished wood seemed artificial from his vantage, like toys for children. People and carts in the narrow streets were as ants. A melancholy smile tugged at Yong Fa's lips. He'd spent most of his life at the Shaolin Temple, but he cherished returning home, seeing loved ones, even though it held a special kind of hurt as well. He always wondered what might have been...

He shook himself, straightened his saffron jacket and the heavy wooden beads around his neck, and started down the winding path. Strong legs and fit lungs made short work of the journey. He passed no one along the way and entered Long-en from the southern end. Villagers paid him the respect due a Buddhist monk, with bows and palms pressed together. Some recognised him and were friendly as well as courteous, but most did not. It had been a long time, after all. Then the old pork bun seller with his rickety cart, who had been supplying the village for longer than Yong Fa had lived, came hurrying up the road, panting and sweating behind his creaking wagon.

"Yong Fa! You're just in time!"

The young monk frowned. "For what?"

"The Jade Dragon!"

"What of it?"

"It's gone!"

Yong Fa's mouth fell open. Their most valuable artefact, the heart of the village for centuries, kept in the temple maintained by his Uncle Bao. "Gone?"

"Stolen! Go, go!" The old man waved a stick-thin arm frantically behind himself, gesturing towards the temple.

Such a theft was unthinkable. Yong Fa thanked the bun seller and hurried away, his pleasure at homecoming shattered.

The temple stood at the centre of the small community, a three-tiered pagoda paying homage to the many gods of agriculture and protection, health and good fortune revered by the local populace. Long-en was a simple place, removed from the bustle of modern life. But one thing set Long-en apart from others of its kind: the Jade Dragon, carved by the master artisan Yao Gailing, five hundred years ago when the area was first settled. Long-en was proud of its history.

A dragon took pity on Yao Gailing, so the story went, as he stumbled through the land, lost, alone and heartbroken. Yao had been in love, his life mapped out, his fortunes grand, until a terrible illness took hold of the woman he loved, and slowly wasted her away. All he sought was a quiet place to live, and peace to mourn his beloved. Yao had no taste for company. The dragon, heart-sick at the man's powerful grief, had split a mountain in two, releasing a small river so that Yao might have his isolation in the peace of the valley. Yao settled there, safe in the arm of stone. In gratitude and homage, Yao fashioned a statue in his saviour's likeness from a boulder of the purest jade that had been washed free from the mountain by that new stream.

Two-feet long, intricately crafted and of the most flawless green, the Jade Dragon was revered by any who saw it. And its auspicious creation and heartfelt intent made it powerful. For centuries it had brought luck and prosperity to Long-en. How the world was changing, Yong Fa thought, if someone would steal such a holy item. And for what? To try to use its powers of protection for themselves? Or even worse, to sell? The theft motivated only for personal gain?

He approached the temple and his cousin, Zi Yi, was the first to spot him. Her face was pale under long black hair tied back in a braid. She wore her trademark olive green *cheongsam* dress. Yong Fa had lived in Long-en for only five years. The first three with parents he no longer remembered, murdered by bandits on the road far from town. One day he had been left with his father's brother, Bao, when his parents travelled to the city far away, for papers. For administrative duties even they could not escape. And they had never returned.

So for two more years Yong Fa lived with

Uncle Bao, Aunt Hua, and precocious Zi Yi, one year older and ten times bossier. Yet to this day, his cousin remained his best friend. His smile broke free at the sight of her. Uncle Bao and Aunt Hua, unable to afford two hungry mouths, had sent him to be raised in the Shaolin Temple when he turned five. He didn't resent them for it, despite the fear and loneliness he had felt keenly at the time. It had given him a better life than he might have hoped for otherwise, but he often wondered...

Zi Yi hugged him tight. "Cousin! Your arrival is fortuitous."

"The bun seller told me. Truly, it's stolen?"

"My father is beside himself. He manned the temple all day yesterday, as usual. He locked up in the evening and returned home." She gestured across the street to the small Li family house. "But this morning, the dragon was gone."

Yong Fa squeezed her arm. "We'll find the thief."

They entered the temple to find Uncle Bao talking urgently with the village elders.

"Nephew!" Bao said. " It is so good to see you, but today is a terrible day."

Yong Fa's expression was hard. "I will track down the culprit."

"There are precious few clues," Bao said. He shook his head. "There's no sign of forced entry. Nothing. It's as if a ghost spirited the Jade Dragon away."

"May I search?" Yong Fa asked.

His uncle gestured widely with both hands. "Be my guest."

"I will continue my own investigation," Zi Yi said, and returned to the temple steps. Yong Fa watched as she removed some icons from the cross-body satchel she habitually wore, filled with the tools of her trade. Her geomantic skills were strong and her ability to commune with spirits unrivalled. While she learned what she could, Yong Fa would investigate the material realm.

He searched among the altars, checked the doors and shuttered windows. All were locked, as Bao had said. The central plinth where the Dragon usually sat was shocking in its nakedness, the blasphemy of the act stark in its absence. The place was immaculately clean, no traces of dirt on the floor, or dust on the furniture. No greasy fingerprints marked the gleaming wood. His Uncle did a superb job of maintaining the temple. Yong Fa sighed and looked up. The second level of the temple was mezzanine-style and the third had no floor, just a row of shuttered windows high above. An open column through the building allowed light in via the slats of all the shutters and showed the conical roof atop the temple, the underside of dull terracotta tiles supported by a hexagon of thick, polished wooden beams.

Yong Fa jogged up the internal stairs on one side and examined the windows there. They were all locked and undisturbed. The next row, some twenty feet above, could only be opened from inside by a long, hooked pole. Yong Fa squinted at a thin line of sunlight leaking crookedly through one of the high shutters.

He leaned over the railing and called down, "I think the thief came from above."

Bao and the elders crowded around Yong Fa as he made his way outside and walked a circle of the outer temple wall.

"Surely no one could scale this building?" Bao said.

Yong Fa grinned. "Let's find out, Uncle!"

He jumped up and caught the lintel of one window and began to climb. Ignoring the cries and admonishments from below, he concentrated on gripping with hardened fingers, relied on intensely trained muscles, and slowly ascended from window to beam to decorative addition. It was an arduous climb, but he made it look easy, until he found himself on the wall of the second floor, squatting on the top of a window frame. He was separated from the third row of shutters high above by smooth wooden boards, offering no handholds at all. The roof flared out over him, six sections of sweeping tile, a sloping polished beam between each one. At the end of each beam, a dragon's head, beautifully carved, watched out over the village in every direction.

Yong Fa paused, closed his eyes, and breathed deeply, using his mastery of the meditative practice of *qi gong* to calm his adrenalised pulse. He exhaled slowly, opened his eyes, concentrating only on the wooden sill of the small window directly above him. With a powerful push of his legs he jumped, stretched, and caught hold of it with confident hands. The gasps and shocked voices from below were as distant as the stars as he focussed only on securing his grip and bracing his feet against the wall. He glanced around, the valley stretched out behind him, pine trees and curling mist.

He spotted the one shutter that was ajar, its ledge scored and gouged as if by a giant bird's claw. The paint was scuffed and scraped where something had been jimmied in the gap between shutter and building to flick the catch.

Yong Fa's grip began to weaken, a tremor in his fingers.

"Uncle Bao," he called. "Could you please unlatch this one?"

Bao nodded, and disappeared inside. A few moments later there was a rattling as the long pole was deployed. "Be careful, Yong Fa!"

The young monk grinned. "I will."

He leaned over, opened the cover, and hauled himself inside to land lightly on the second floor. His Shaolin-trained skills made the drop easy.

"You've always been a risk taker," Uncle Bao said with a frown. "Even when you were a baby before your parents..." Uncle Bao smiled sadly. "You gave them the run around, eh? And then me and your Aunt Hua."

"I know my limits, Uncle. This was well within them."

"Have you learned anything from your crazy acrobatics?"

Yong Fa smiled ruefully. "These windows

here," he indicated the second floor, "are locked with a hasp, but those above have a simple hook, because no one can get to them, after all. They don't even really need to be locked, the hook simply to prevent them banging in the wind?"

"Quite so," Bao said.

"Well, someone managed to get a grapple onto the window from outside and used a knife or similar to flick open that hook. They would have lowered themselves inside with a rope, I imagine, and escaped the same way, with the Jade Dragon. Except the damage their grapple made to the wood meant they couldn't close the shutter properly."

Bao used his pole to pull the shutter in and, indeed, it sat a little crooked in the frame.

"Whoever stole the dragon knew this temple well," Yong Fa said.

Zi Yi, long accustomed to ignoring the noise of the world around her, sat in meditation. She was glad her crazy cousin was here, though who knew what he was up to. She let her mind's eye wander the valley, circling gently outwards from the temple. Not far away, above the house of the local herbalist, a disturbance in the ether caught her attention. She respectfully acknowledged it.

"Greetings, Seeker," the spirit whispered,

its voice like a summer breeze through tall grass.

"Greetings," she returned, and waited patiently, politely, her astral form hovering.

"We may converse if you wish," the spirit said.

"Thank you. Were you here through the night?"

"Nearby."

"And did you see any activity around our temple?"

"I saw your dragon leave."

Zi Yi's heart quickened. She needed to be careful with her wording, capricious as elemental spirits were, they often preferred games to simple facts. "Mighty Wind Spirit, master of all the air," she said, buttering it up, "did you see who our dragon left with?"

"Of course."

"Who was it?"

"Why should I tell you?"

"Kindness?" Zi Yi suggested.

"Why would you think me kind?"

Never would a spirit give anything, even the simplest of news, without exacting a price.

"What favour might I offer?" Zi Yi asked. In her thirty-one years she had racked up a sizeable debt of this sort, but luckily not many had yet come to claim their due. Those who had gave her nothing but trouble. But this was how the game was played.

The element danced in the air, formless but showing ripples like clouds reflected in water disturbed by a stone. "I need nothing from you, tiny flesh." The conversation was clearly over.

Zi Yi sighed. "Very well. Thank you for your time."

She pulled her spectral form away from the soft zephyr of laughter and pushed her perception along the main road out of the village. Several crows sat on one rooftop, cawing lazily. Opening her physical eyes, she looked through the real world at the dark birds. She pulled some fine paper, thin as hope, from her satchel and carefully crafted it, fold after fold until she held a tiny simulacrum of a corvid on her palm. She tapped it once on the head and whispered, "Crow Spirit, to me."

With a shiver, the paper bird flapped its wings once and cocked its head to eye her.

"Thank you for coming," she said with a smile. She nodded up to the birds on the eaves down the street. "Your friends might have seen someone leaving in the night. Someone with our jade dragon?"

"They might," Crow Spirit replied cautiously.

"Could you describe the person?"

"He wore burgundy spun with threads of gold. The top of his head shone in the moonlight. He had a toxic *shen*, unkind."

Zi Yi frowned. Such a description might fit any number of people. "Could your friends fly now, find him, tell me where he's going?"

"They could," Crow Spirit said. "But why would they?"

Zi Yi smiled. "I would owe you a favour if you help me until the man is found and our property returned to us."

Crow Spirit hopped from paper foot to foot as he considered her offer. "I owe Fox Spirit a life."

Zi Yi's eyes widened. "A life?"

"A rabbit meal we stole from her, that she means to collect. Present Fox Spirit with the debt I owe her and your favour will be granted. I'll stay with you until the man you seek is found."

Zi Yi carefully kept her relief hidden. This bargain came cheaply. The interests of animal spirits often seemed laughable, but they drew no distinction between a rabbit or a man or a village, so it was ever wise to be cautious. "Very well," she said. "I will supply a rabbit life for Fox Spirit."

"And we will watch this man for you."

2

Yong Fa and Zi Yi were explaining all they had learned to the elders when a rustling came from Zi Yi's bag. She pulled forth the tiny paper crow and listened to its report. "The man has made his way to Nanjing Bay," she said.

"Who is the thief?" her father asked, casting an eye of wonder towards the form perched on her palm.

"I have no way of knowing. They don't draw a distinction between people any more than we do between separate crows, but they recognise his attire."

The paper crow hopped to her shoulder, and Zi Yi pulled her *luopan* from her satchel. She began adjusting the multiple dials of the geomantic compass, aligning characters and symbols as she turned slowly in a circle on the spot. "If I had more to go on," she said, "my grandmother's treasure here could surely track him." She shook her head, and returned what was far more than a simple tool of *feng shui* to her bag. With a word of thanks to the paper crow she gently folded it flat and tucked it away. "But I need more information."

"What can this criminal hope to gain?" Uncle Bao asked.

"He wouldn't try to sell our dragon in the city, surely?" one of the elders asked.

Zi Yi shook her head. "I'll wager the fool plans to use its influence for his own selfish gains. The dragon has brought our village health and good fortune for hundreds of years. I imagine he wishes to harness that power."

"Is such a thing even possible?" Uncle Bao asked. "Isn't the icon tied to us, its power befitting this place?"

"Honestly, Father, I don't know," Zi Yi said.

"Regardless," Yong Fa said. "I'll track him down and return the dragon to its rightful place. It is Long-en's treasure and in Long-en it should stay."

"*We* will, cousin," Zi Yi said. "We go together and we go now. He has a long head start."

Yong Fa bowed respectfully. "Very well. I'm ready."

Zi Yi nodded. "Just give me ten minutes. I just have to fetch a rabbit from the market and leave it by the river."

The cousins set off to the south in a companionable silence. Yong Fa enjoyed the sweet pine scent of the cool air. He was confident they would find the thief, but he worried a little for Zi Yi. She had taken the robbery personally as if it had somehow besmirched her own reputation. Her family was responsible for the temple, after all, yet he knew his cousin well enough not to push the matter or try to assuage her concerns. Her resentment would be fuel, either for their journey or an argument, and he knew very well which he would rather.

They walked for several hours before choosing a spot in the shade to rest and eat. Both their bags were heavy with gifts of food from the village. They unwrapped sticky rice rolls, and passed a skin of water back and forth.

Eventually, Yong Fa broke the quiet. "A shame such a fine day should be spoiled with this business."

"What if we fail?" Zi Yi said.

"What?"

"If we can't recover the dragon, what then?"

"We will, cousin, never fear."

"Yong Fa, you can't be certain! If we fail, what will become of the village?"

The monk smiled softly. "It's true it has brought great fortune for a long time, but the village is populated with wonderful people like you and your family. Long-en's prosperity depends on warm people, not cold stone statues."

"It is also populated by greedy fools like the one who robbed us."

"They are not so common," Yong Fa said. "Besides, the gentle way is to forgive the disreputable for their flaws. Your forgiveness will reach out, so they can be filled with it, embraced by it, and better themselves."

"I will not forgive this bandit!" Zi Yi said hotly.

"Perhaps not. But your kindness can help others. This thief is one bad apple and we'll deal with him."

Zi Yi narrowed her eyes at her cousin. "You contradict yourself."

Yong Fa grinned. "I am an imperfect man."

"You left at five years old and never grew up!" Zi Yi said. "I can imagine what a nightmare you were for the Abbot and your teachers."

"Of course I was! I also studied very hard and did them proud. But I can't be serious all the time, and I cannot deny my own flaws."

"You're a good man." Zi Yi smiled gently and opened her mouth to say more but was interrupted by a flurry of wings as a dark shape fluttered by to catch her attention. She carefully removed the paper crow from her satchel and it hopped onto her finger. "What news?" she asked.

The spirit's message passed into her mind and Zi Yi frowned.

"Not good news," she reported. "The man has boarded a boat and set sail. Crow Spirit has told me his direction, but they can follow him no further."

"To sea? Where is he headed, I wonder?"

"They tell me of a teahouse, where he made his plans. The ship is very large. I think he intends to travel far. We can ask around when we reach the port."

They continued on and when they reached the Huangmao River a friendly fisherman agreed to ferry them to Nanjing Bay for a rather ridiculous sum. Zi Yi protested, but Yong Fa convinced her that haste outweighed the need to bargain. Many villagers had donated kindly to their endeavour, he reminded her, they could share a little of that generosity. She sulked in the back of the boat all the way, while Yong Fa tried to hide his grin.

Despite his exorbitant fee, the fisherman refused to get too close to the busy port, and dropped them half an hour's walk away. Zi Yi shot Yong Fa a venomous look as they started along the riverbank, but he simply smiled. The road was dusty and busy with carts, travellers and traders, but the journey was uneventful. Yong Fa's saffron robes demanded respect and Zi Yi's scowl took care of anything else. They rode a ferry across the narrow strait to the small island and walked the last half mile or so to Nanjing among thickening crowds. The day grew long and twilight bathed the land.

The noise of hawkers and the rattle of wagons in the narrow streets made conversation difficult. The smell of incense and cooking, rice wine and herbs, saturated the air. Zi Yi leaned close, pointed and said, "That's what the crow showed me."

Yong Fa looked at the ramshackle teahouse and frowned. "The thief made his travel arrangements there?"

"Apparently."

They entered the low building and several eyebrows were raised at the sight of a monk with a well-dressed young woman. No amount of religious respect or scowling could turn those stares away. Zi Yi drew herself up and refused to meet a single gaze as she made her way to the counter at the back.

The tea seller bowed, a smile plastered on his lips that animated no other part of his face. "Tea?" he asked uselessly.

"A man was here this morning," Zi Yi said. "Bald on top, red and gold *changshan*, carrying a rather large parcel, I would imagine."

The tea seller's eyes narrowed. "I don't remember such a man."

Zi Yi leaned forward, threatening. "Yes, you do."

The vendor was momentarily taken aback. "What of it? What's it to you?"

"He organised passage from here. Where to?"

The tea seller laughed, suddenly relaxed, and flapped one hand. "Fly away little bird, this is no place for you."

Yong Fa bristled, the hairs on his neck standing up. Something had changed. Not only in the tea seller's demeanour, but in the shop in general. A quiet had settled. Trusting his instincts, he ducked and turned as a stout club whistled through the air where his head had been a moment before. The man wielding it was momentarily shocked and Yong Fa felled him with two quick, iron hard punches to the sternum. Four more thugs stepped up and the fight was on.

Patrons scrambled out of the way, dragging tables with them, desperate to avoid flying limbs and chairs. Yong Fa's skills were legion, but four on one was tough odds. He dodged left and right, dropped, and swept the feet from under one attacker, rose quickly to kick another hard in the chest. That one flew backwards over a table and smashed out through wooden shutters into the dusty street. A sword cleaved the air and Yong Fa stepped forward, one hand up to intercept the swinging arm. The blade stopped mere inches from his neck, and Yong Fa's palm strike exploded the swordsman's nose. The man staggered backwards, his chest a scarlet waterfall.

"Outside! Outside!" screamed the tea seller, but the fighters had no ears for courtesy.

As the swept man tried to rise, Zi Yi smashed a heavy teapot onto his head and he collapsed bonelessly. Yong Fa spun forward, finished off the swordsman even as another stepped in with a knife. The monk's robes parted at the razor edge, just below his ribs, but his skin escaped thanks to fancy footwork. Yong Fa grabbed the wrist of the knife arm, twisted it and kicked the man's knee. He fell screaming with his arm broken and his knee dislocated.

"This way!" A lithe young man with a thin face beckoned from the doorway. "More are coming! Hurry!"

3

The cousins exchanged a glance, shrugged, and ran from the teahouse, following the young man left and right through the vibrant streets. After several turns he hopped onto a low shed, causing the chickens inside to burst into a flurry of apoplexy, and shimmied nimbly up a downpipe to the tile roof two stories above the road. As Yong Fa and Zi Yi scrambled up behind, he turned a bright grin to them.

"My name is Lau," he said. "We'll be safe up here if we stay low."

Yong Fa bowed, but before he could speak Zi Yi said, "Why did you save us?"

"You were in trouble."

"We didn't need saving."

Lau laughed. "Oh, you did. Do you know who you were fighting?"

Zi Yi chose not to answer and Yong Fa was pleased to see her caution. "Who?" he asked.

"Crimson Cloud *tong*! You have made powerful enemies today."

"But they attacked us!" Zi Yi said.

"You asked questions in the wrong places. That teahouse is their territory."

Yong Fa frowned. "What do they care if we ask about a traveller in their teahouse?"

"Who were you asking about?"

"A man from our village," Yong Fa said. "We simply enquired after a shaven-headed man in burgundy and gold, who made travel plans there today."

Lau's eyebrows rose. "You asked about Bak Ma? He's a Crimson Cloud Red Pole."

"Bak Ma?" Zi Yi spat in shock. "I know him from our village, he made a living like me, geomancy, *feng shui*, divination services, but he travelled a lot. And unlike me, he's a fraud! He preys on the weak and vulnerable."

"That may be so," Lau said. "But he's a Crimson Cloud Red Pole nonetheless."

"What is that?" Yong Fa asked.

"A *tong* Enforcer. Lowest are the uninitiated, the Blue Lanterns, then there are Forty-Nines, then Red Poles. He answers to the Deputy Mountain Master."

"He's Triad?" Zi Yi said, incredulous.

"Yes."

"How do you know so much?" Zi Yi asked.

Lau smiled. "I've seen him there often, drinking tea and wine, trading goods and insults in equal measure." He touched a finger to his ear, then the corner of his eye. "I keep my ear to the gossip and my eyes open. Crimson Cloud have been terrorising this place forever, my useless father pays them a fortune in protection. I'll never inherit his business because it'll belong to them before long. My father and I are great disappointments to each other."

"That's a sad story," Yong Fa said. "You should try to repair relations."

"Not interested. Either of us."

"And we don't have time for counselling,

Yong Fa!" Zi Yi snapped.

"It seems all my spying and watchfulness has paid off," Lau said.

"How?"

"You want Bak Ma. I want out of here. We can do a deal."

"Really? What can you offer?" Zi Yi asked.

Lau grinned broadly. "I know where Bak Ma went."

Zi Yi grabbed at his shirt. "Tell us! Now! Enough of these games."

Lau held up both palms, warding the geomancer back. "No, my information has a cost. I have no money. I can get you on Bak Ma's trail, but you take me and pay my passage. That's my price."

Yong Fa and Zi Yi exchanged a glance. "It's a deal," Zi Yi said with a sigh.

Lau clapped. "Yes! Bak Ma's ship has sailed, but if we're quick, we can get on the next one out. There won't be another going for some weeks."

"Which ship?" Zi Yi asked.

Lau shook his head. "I'm no fool, you'll leave me behind! We go together." He crept forward to peek over the roof's edge. "The place will be crawling with Crimson Cloud looking for you."

"We'll be careful," Yong Fa said.

"No, no, they'll question everyone."

"They can't possibly!" Zi Yi scoffed.

"They are many, and their spies are everywhere."

Night had settled over the town. Yong Fa looked down into the inky street, still bustling, though less so than before. There was a new moon and not much starlight. The buildings were brightly lit inside by candles and lanterns, but their roofs were shrouded in darkness. "Let's go over the top then," he said. "We're all fit and capable. The port is not so far." He pointed across to the roof opposite. "With a run up, you could both jump that gap, couldn't you?"

"We could try," Zi Yi said. "How many streets to cross between here and the boat?" she asked Lau.

The young man paused, eyes closed in thought. Eventually he said, "You know, if we move along on this side all the way to the cobbler, we would only have to jump two narrow streets." He hurried away.

"You'll get us killed one of these days," Zi Yi complained to her cousin.

"Me? Maybe if you'd been polite in the teahouse we wouldn't be sneaking across rooftops like cats," Yong Fa said, and ducked a slap.

In a crouching run, they hurried after the young man. Yong Fa's years of training ensured he was silent as the moon, but both Zi Yi and Lau impressed him. They made noise, but very little, and certainly not enough to be heard from below. When they reached the end of the tight row of buildings, Lau pointed.

"We need to be over there," he said. "You can see the port from here."

Tall masts and sails and the bulks of

steamers were solid silhouettes in the distance. Lights burned here and there, candles and oil lamps on wagons and in windows and on the handcarts of street vendors.

Yong Fa glanced below. No one seemed to be paying attention to the roofs. He took a couple of steps back then ran and easily leaped across the narrow street. Almost immediately, Lau landed lightly beside him. "You move well," he told the young man.

"Not as well as you!"

"Keep at it and you will."

"I can't do it!" Zi Yi said, her voice a harsh whisper of frustration.

"You can!" Yong Fa said.

Zi Yi's face was twisted in frustration. Yong Fa knew she was angry at herself, unable to master the fear that glued her feet to the tiles. He leapt back across.

"Get on my back."

She looked at him as though he had just grown an ox from his forehead. "What?"

"I'll carry you. You're only a little woman."

Zi Yi's mouth fell open and her eyes hardened. She turned away, then ran and launched herself across. Thankfully Lau was there to grab her hand as she teetered on the edge of the roof.

Yong Fa landed beside her, grinning.

"You are a contemptible man and have no right to call yourself a monk," Zi Yi said.

"It worked, didn't it?"

She shook her head and stalked away.

"Quickly," Lau said. "Before someone sees or

hears us."

They hurried after Zi Yi and were soon at the end of another row of buildings. Visible only one street away was the port, a bustling, restless place, even in darkness. People pushed wagons loaded with goods to and fro, the odour of the ocean, seaweed and engine fuel for the steamers was ripe in the air. The next gap they needed to jump was too wide. The three stood back in the gloom and looked at their destination. So near and yet so far.

"Honestly, I'm not sure even I could make that," Yong Fa said.

Zi Yi snorted. "You're lying. You could easily make that and more. But neither Lau nor I could."

"I don't remember this street being so wide," Lau said.

"Then there's nothing else for it. We climb down and take our chances." Zi Yi's eyes challenged them to contradict her.

A ruckus below caught their attention as one group of men pushed and shoved another. There were harsh words and blows exchanged.

"Those on the left are Crimson Cloud," Lau whispered, retreating from the edge. "They grow frustrated that they can't find you, I imagine. And over there, see? There's more. And those three by the noodle seller are Crimson Cloud Forty-Nines."

"The whole port is crawling with the bastards," Zi Yi spat.

Lau pointed to a dark gap between buildings. "The quickest way is through there. See that big auxiliary steamer? That's our vessel, the *Northern Belle*. We don't have long, she sails in under an hour."

"So what do we do?" Zi Yi asked.

Lau sniffed. "I'm going to cause a distraction. When I catch their attention, you two run. Once you're on board, you're safe, assuming you get there unseen. I'll lose them and join you."

"And if you don't make it in time?" Yong Fa asked.

"A risk I'll have to take."

"Why are you willing to do so much for us?" Zi Yi asked.

Lau laughed. "If you'd spent more than a few hours here, you'd understand my need to escape. Trust me, it's worth the risk. Don't miss your chance!"

With that, he hurried away and dropped out of sight.

"And we still don't know what else he knew of Bak Ma's plans," Zi Yi said, her voice tight.

Yong Fa shrugged. "Then let's hope he makes it back. If not, perhaps we'll learn more on the ship. At least we'll know where Bak Ma has gone if our ship is going there too, as Lau said it was."

They crept to the edge and looked over. The thugs were still pushing people around down below. Lau's voice rang out. "A Shaolin monk is fighting near Auntie Mai's!"

"Our signal, you think?" Yong Fa asked with a grin.

The crowds surged away from the harbour.

"No arguments," Yong Fa said. "You must trust me." He dropped two stories to land light as a cat, then held out his arms. "I'll catch you!"

"Damn you!" Zi Yi said. She closed her eyes and jumped.

Yong Fa braced for the impact and caught his cousin with a small grunt. He set her down and they ran. Stepping into the lantern light, they hurried across the open harbour, dodging wagons and oxen left and right to quickly reach the gangplank to the ship. Two men holding large knives stepped out of the shadows of a stack of crates.

"Not so fast," one said. "We're not so easily fooled."

The cousins skidded to a halt.

"We used our brains, see. This is the only other ship leaving for Australia, so of course you'd try to get aboard if you're following Bak Ma."

"Australia?" Zi Yi whispered.

Yong Fa decided not to converse. He hammered out a kick, taking the talkative thug under the chin. The man flipped over the gangplank and hit the dark water to sink like a stone. As his partner shot forward, Yong Fa blocked the man's knife hand, stepped past and used the attacker's momentum to turn him. Yong Fa palmed the staggering man's head into the railing of the gang plank, felling him with a dull *thwack*.

"We can't let them report, at least not until the ship is away," Yong Fa said. He looked into the bay. "I don't think that one is coming back."

Zi Yi pointed at the unattended crates the villains had hidden behind. Yong Fa hauled bolts of cloth out of one not yet sealed, tossing the merchandise into the harbour, and hefted the senseless man into the empty wooden box, working quickly in the shadows the cargo provided. As the man began to murmur and come around, Yong Fa placed the lid and punched each nail into place with accurate, single-knuckle strikes. Then he lifted another crate on top as dull thudding began.

"Have a good trip!" Yong Fa said to the box.

They glanced around to ensure no-one had paid any mind to the brief fracas, then strolled casually back into the lantern light and up the gangplank. They were met by a swarthy sailor with a scarlet birthmark from brow to chin across one side of his face. "Help you?"

"Your captain, is he here?"

The man pointed out a burly European with a barrel chest and a mass of wild red hair. Yong Fa approached him. "Excuse me. We wish to arrange passage with you."

The captain peered down at the young monk. "Cutting it fine," he said in heavily-accented Mandarin. "We leave on the tide in fifteen minutes."

"Just in time then," Yong Fa said with a broad smile.

When the captain told Zi Yi the fare she bit her

tongue and paid. "Our friend, a young man called Lau, should join us any moment," she said. "I'll pay for him, too."

The captain shrugged. "As you wish. But if he's not here, I won't wait. See Gilly about your cabin. You'll all be sharing." He strode away.

"Australia!" Zi Yi said. "That's months at sea!"

Yong Fa nodded, lips pursed. "But what choice do we have if that's where the Jade Dragon has been taken?"

They waited in shadows on the deck to avoid being seen and watched the harbour for Lau, but fifteen minutes later the steamer left Nanjing Bay without him.

"I feel bad," Yong Fa said. "He risked everything and helped us only to be left behind."

"And we've only got half his information!" Zi Yi said. Her eyes narrowed and she ran to the rail. "Wait, though. Look!"

Lau came pelting across the dock, dancing obstacles left and right. Without slowing he dove from the wharf and hit the water with barely a splash. Moments later he surfaced, swimming hard. Yong Fa heaved a mooring rope to the side, grunting with effort as he lowered the thick, heavy cord to trail in the ship's increasing wake.

"He'll never make it!" Zi Yi exclaimed, but Lau swam like a fish and snagged a hold of the lifeline.

Yong Fa hauled and Lau climbed. Zi Yi held

her cousin's waist and finally Lau fell over the rail, gasping.

He staggered to his feet and grinned, his face bruised, left arm bleeding.

"By the Emperor in Heaven, you made it!" Yong Fa said.

"Only just!" Lau replied.

Yong Fa patted his shoulder. "Are you badly hurt? What happened?"

"A little battered and one of them got a knife to me, but it's not too bad. Once I led them away, and they realised I was lying, they got angry. I swore I'd told the truth, but they beat me anyhow. I managed to get away before they did too much damage, ran the long way back and saw the ship already leaving."

"You could not have cut it finer, but what an effort you made!" Yong Fa said, genuinely impressed.

They leaned against the ship's rail, Lau getting his breath back, and watched the dancing oil lamps of night fishing boats that scurried away from the large steamer. Before long they were in open water, land lost in the darkened distance. They went in search of Gilly who showed them their cabin, which was little more than a large cupboard with pallets and sacking for beds.

Lau looked about. "Three of us and only two berths."

"We can share sleeping on the floor between them, you and I," Yong Fa said. "It won't be so bad."

Lau grinned. "Not at all. I'm away from Nanjing

Bay, that's all that matters to me!"

There would be no more stops until Singapore, they'd been told, then Surabaya, and then a long haul to Sydney, Melbourne and, finally Adelaide. "You'll need to stay on board in Sydney and Melbourne," Gilly had said. "Chinese are restricted in Australia now, you won't get in without licences, which I'm sure you don't have. But if you wait until Adelaide, you can slip in and trek back to the goldfields from there. I assume that's where you're headed."

"Now tell us more," Zi Yi said to Lau. "Is Bak Ma going all the way to Australia? Do you know where? And why?"

"He's got a plan to make a fortune," Lau said. "That's why Crimson Cloud were happy to finance his passage. There's gold in Australia, mountains of it for the taking, if you believe the stories."

"I'm not sure I do," Zi Yi said.

"With Crimson Cloud influence, Bak Ma secured a visa to enter via Melbourne," Lau went on. "But as Gilly said, we'll need to go to Adelaide. It's a trek on foot, some two hundred and fifty miles across unforgiving terrain to the goldfields."

"You seem to know an awful lot about this place," Zi Yi said suspiciously.

"I told you," Lau replied. "I watch and I listen."

"This journey is becoming more horrifying by the second," moaned Zi Yi.

"Ah, but worth it for the fortunes to be made!" said Lau, grinning widely.

"This is not a game, Lau. Bak Ma has a lot to answer for. And he'll have a huge head start on us, possibly months before we finally reach wherever he's headed."

"You're sure that's his plan?" Yong Fa asked.

Lau nodded emphatically. "I was in the teahouse when Bak Ma was making his case. He told the Crimson Cloud bosses he could get his hands on an artefact that would guarantee success and ensure he gained control of the richest mine. He promised to harvest great wealth, and send back huge sums to repay the *tong's* investment in him a thousand times over. He planned to establish the society there as well, to ensure they have a powerful presence early in the new land."

"So that's his game," Zi Yi said. "To use the power of Yao Gailing's jade masterpiece for his own gain and the wealth of criminals. He's despicable!"

"We'll stop him," Yong Fa said. "You have your friends to help, yes?"

Zi Yi retrieved the fragile paper crow from her bag and it hopped into life. Ignoring Lau's gasp, she asked, "Can you help us?"

"Only back on land," Crow Spirit replied. "We are not sea-faring birds." It sounded genuinely apologetic.

Zi Yi passed on its message, carefully returning the creature to her satchel.

"Can your *luopan* assist, now you know who

we seek?" Yong Fa wondered.

Zi Yi nodded and took the compass from her bag. She adjusted it and thought of Bak Ma. Her will controlled the magic inside and it responded immediately, though weakly. "The trouble is, there's no real accuracy over distances like these," she said. "But as we get closer, it'll be more useful."

"Where does Bak Ma think these great riches are to be found?" Yong Fa asked.

Lau grinned. The young man seemed to show his teeth a lot. "It's called Ballarat."

"What a thoroughly horrible sounding place," Zi Yi said.

"Your mood is dark because of the task ahead of us," Yong Fa said. "Understandably so. But we have our goal and our cause is just." He asked Lau, "There's no chance our ship will catch up to his?"

"No," Lau said, his smile fading for once. "His vessel sails directly to Sydney, then Melbourne. That's why he chose it. We have to make stops, so even with the best weather in the world we'll be several weeks behind."

4

The days aboard ship soon became a drudgery of routine. Meagre food rations shared with the crew, picking up as much English as they could from anyone who would teach them, endless games of *mah jong* on deck to while away the hours. Yong Fa trained in any open space he could find, always watched by the crew and other passengers, mesmerised and entertained by his high energy martial forms. He would meditate frequently, and, when asked, happily share his learnings about Buddhism, the martial arts, or *qi gong*. After a while, by popular demand, he led regular morning practice for sailors and passengers alike. Some simply enjoyed the novelty of it, others realised they had discovered a unique and privileged opportunity in a passenger with Yong Fa's skills. He hoped at least some of them would further their study once the journey was over.

Meanwhile, Zi Yi busied herself with esoteric study, and conversed with the spirits as much as with human company. She preferred the spirits, and Yong Fa knew she struggled with the close proximity of so many others. In normal life, Zi Yi would spend hours or even days, alone in the forests around Long-en. Alone from people, at least, but in commune with the animals and spirits with whom she shared far more understanding. Yong Fa hoped the confines of the ship weren't too much of a strain on her. It was a long journey, after all.

Lau became friendly with many of the crew. He was a quiet and polite lodger in their cramped cabin, and refused to let Yong Fa take the floor, insisting the monk always sleep on the pallet. He helped around ship to keep busy and the captain and crew seemed to tolerate him with good humour.

Other than enduring the occasional frightening storm, they simply waited as miles of ocean slipped beneath them.

The boredom of shipboard life was broken only when they made port. In Singapore and Surabaya they enjoyed a little time on land visiting markets and spending some of their coin in restaurants, eating far too much simply because the food wasn't their usual on-board rations. Zi Yi bought exotic fruits and vegetables to supplement their otherwise bland diet.

One morning, a week from Sydney, Zi Yi rose before dawn. Her sleep had been troubled for reasons she couldn't fathom and after a night of restless shifting about on the coarse bedding, she gave up and crept from the cabin while the men slumbered on. She strolled the deck in the indigo of pre-dawn, the breeze cool and salty as it lifted her hair. She found a secluded spot at the rail, took the *luopan* from her satchel and set to adjusting the dials. She felt the instrument tune in with her will, her overwhelming desire to find that bastard, Bak Ma. He was somewhere out there. The *luopan* pointed a little due west of their heading, so nothing had changed.

The compass was snatched from her grasp by a thin hand. Zi Yi spun around to face the thief and paused for a moment, stunned to see Lau standing there. She thought for a moment it was a joke, but his open, happy face was closed and mean. He held her *luopan* in one hand and slapped her hard with the other.

"My patience had almost run out," he said as she staggered, ears ringing with the blow. "I've been waiting weeks for this chance!"

Blood trickled from Zi Yi's split lip. "What are you doing?" she asked, her voice slurred.

"Crimson Cloud think I'm unworthy, do they? Won't let me join, eh?" Lau said, teeth bared. "I've shown them!" He hefted the *luopan*. "When I present this to Bak Ma as proof I succeeded where the rest of Crimson Cloud failed, he'll make me his right hand."

Zi Yi tried to rally herself and Lau backhanded her, made her stagger again. Close to passing out, she grabbed for the rail and missed, fell to her knees. "Lau, no..."

"Don't worry, you won't be alone for long. Your worthless cousin will soon follow."

Zi Yi tried to focus, to gather some kind of equilibrium. She cried out, but her voice was nothing more than a croak. As she drew a deep breath, determined to scream until the entire ship awoke, Lau grabbed under her arms and hefted her up before the sound left her lips.

The young man's lithe form belied his

considerable strength and he threw her over the rail. Her scream escaped all too late as Lau's leering face retreated from her at speed and she hit the cold waves hard.

Yong Fa awoke to shouts and the pounding of rushing feet in the corridors. He sat up and saw that neither Zi Yi nor Lau were in the cabin with him. His heart hammered, suddenly sure that something was terribly wrong. He ran up to the deck to see a crowd arguing back and forth, Lau among them.

The captain, a hulking presence in the centre of the group, threw both his hands up and shouted, "It's too late! Simple as that." He repeated himself in several languages, none of which Yong Fa understood, then strode away.

Lau turned, his expression a picture of misery, and saw Yong Fa. He pushed his way through the press of bodies. "Oh, such awful news. I'm so sorry!"

"What's happened?"

"It's Zi Yi. She's lost overboard."

Yong Fa's stomach became liquid, his legs shook. "What?"

"A crewman heard a scream, saw her floundering in the ship's wake, but by the time the alarm had been raised, we had sailed too far."

Yong Fa shook his head, refusing to believe it. "We have to turn the ship around!"

Lau's shoulders slumped. "That's what I told the captain, and half the crew insisted too, but he refused. He says even if we did turn about, there's no way to find one lost soul in this open ocean."

Gilly approached them, shaking his head. "I'm sorry, but the captain's right. We'd never find her. And there are sharks, which are sure to reach her well before we do. A terrible loss. I'm sorry, Yong Fa. Sometimes this happens, life at sea is dangerous."

"No," the monk said. "This can't be."

"I'm sorry." The man moved off, head hung low.

"How could she go overboard?" Yong Fa asked Lau. "She's fit, smart, strong. These sides are higher than her waist. It's inconceivable."

"She was out of the cabin before dawn. I heard her tossing and turning last night. Perhaps she was so tired that she fell asleep leaning on the rail?"

Yong Fa turned away, his mind reeling. How could his cousin be gone, so quickly, so utterly? Tears breached his eyes and he stalked to the stern to be alone.

He took refuge in a vigorous training routine, trying to assuage his frustration, but all he managed to do was exhaust his body. He returned to the cabin, lay down on his pallet, and let nightmare-filled sleep take him rather than remain conscious any longer.

5

Zi Yi awoke cold and wet. Something rose and fell rhythmically beneath her. Everywhere was black and her face hurt. Her mind reeled, tried to make sense of the darkness, the cold, the undulating movements. Disorientation made her nauseated. Slowly she picked out bright points in the darkness and realised they were stars.

Her memory flooded back. She sat up in shock, and fell into the sea. She gasped, gagged, spat out saltwater, and flailed. She was not a strong swimmer. Once again, something nudged her from below and lifted her free of the wet embrace. She held tight to smooth, grey skin, and one shiny black eye tipped back to look at her. A pod of dolphins circled around, occasionally darting away only to return and watch once more.

"You've been asleep a long time," Dolphin Spirit said.

"Thank you for catching me."

"You have little chance of surviving my realm. Why did you enter it?"

Zi Yi laughed. "It was unintentional! An evil man tried to drown me."

Dolphin Spirit clicked rapidly to his pod and they danced and ducked. "Would you have me save you?" he asked.

"You already have."

"But I'm under no obligation to continue doing so."

Zi Yi sighed. So fickle, these spirits. "If I asked you to return me to the ship from where I fell, what would you ask of me?"

"I caught you because I saw power in you," Dolphin Spirit said. "Return to me someone I've lost and I'll return you to those who have lost you."

It sounded like one of those bigger favours. "Who?"

"A maiden who was fish in the water, but walked on two legs on land. When she would visit the waves, we were lovers. I never begrudged her the time she spent on the sands, but one day she didn't return."

Zi Yi considered the spirit's words. "You're talking about a mermaid," she said eventually. "Truly, you knew such a creature?"

"I did. And we loved each other. She would not choose to abandon me, I am sure."

Though she felt almost certain she would live to regret it, Zi Yi nodded. "Very well. I should warn you, I'm on a journey that will take many moons. But I promise that when it is done I will call on you and do all I can to help. Is that acceptable to you?"

There was a surge in the water, several dolphins swarming a sharper shape with a steeper fin that switched in the waves and fled. Zi Yi realised the circling pod was keeping sharks away. Coldness seeped into her gut.

Dolphin Spirit clicked and ducked. "We have an agreement."

"Can you catch up to my ship?"

"We've been trailing it since you hit the water.

We can overtake it before the next time the sun dives. Hold tight."

Zi Yi leaned forward to grasp Dolphin Spirit's pectoral fins, and the animal leaped and powered off through the waves. Zi Yi squinted her eyes against the spray. She was repeatedly dunked, then raised leaping long enough to catch her breath before diving briefly beneath the surface once more. She braced herself for a long, arduous ride.

As the sun sank Yong Fa stood at the stern of the steamer, looking into the past. Back that way his cousin had been alive. Back there, the Jade Dragon was in its rightful place, the village was peaceful and prosperous, no clouds covered the moon. Now, everything was shrouded in darkness. He had tried to remain personally unburdened by the theft, had attempted to cool Zi Yi's vengeful fire, but he was an imperfect man. Everything had changed. He vowed to destroy Bak Ma, in his cousin's name, and return the icon to the temple.

A soft scuff of shoe on deck drew his attention from the darkening sky. Lau, again. He refused to turn around. Twice the night before he had woken to the young man stalking about their cabin. Overcome with grief, he claimed, at Zi Yi's tragic death.

But something disquieted Yong Fa and he couldn't pin it down. He walked the decks, fuming. For only two days his cousin had been gone, yet it felt as if the pain of it would never ease. *His* turmoil was indeed grief. But something about Lau's disposition was off. The young man discomfited him in a new way, something about the youth's demeanour changed, hardened.

"Leave me be," he said, glancing over his shoulder. His eyes narrowed at the young man's grunt of surprise, and was that a flash of silver he saw, sliding into Lau's tunic? A knife? Yong Fa's nerves sang, his body tensed in readiness. He took a long, deep breath, centring and steadying himself.

"I... I... wanted to see you were okay," Lau said.

"What are you doing?" Yong Fa asked, turning to face the young man. His disquiet had grown to full blown suspicion.

Lau's eyes grew wide as plates and he staggered backwards. "No, no, no!" he muttered, as colour drained from his face.

Yong Fa realised the young man was looking past him. The monk sidestepped and turned to see a bedraggled creature, wild wet hair and furious eyes, teeth bared, haul itself up over the gunwale. His shock washed away in a sea of relief as he recognised Zi Yi.

"Grab him!" she said as she jumped to the deck.

Lau squealed and turned to run, but Yong Fa was too fast.

"My *luopan*!" Zi Yi growled. "Where is it?"

Lau dropped to his knees and scrabbled in his satchel, whimpering. He pulled out the enchanted *feng shui* compass. "I'm sorry, you have to understand…"

He didn't get to finish the sentence as Zi Yi snatched away her treasure, then kicked him hard. Several teeth scattered across the deck and Lau collapsed to lie still.

"Throw him overboard," Zi Yi said, her voice cold.

"But, cousin…"

Zi Yi hissed and pushed Yong Fa aside. With strength born of fury she grabbed Lau's jacket and slung him, in one movement, up onto the ship's rail. For all his wiry strength, Lau was small and light.

"No!" Yong Fa shouted.

But it was too late. Zi Yi heaved and Lau's limp form dropped from sight.

The cousins stared at each other for a long moment, then fell into a strong embrace.

"I thought I'd lost you!" Yong Fa said into her wet hair.

"I'm not that easily lost," she said.

"Let's get you below and dry," Yong Fa said. "And you can tell me just how in heaven you survived!"

As they headed below deck, Yong Fa glanced back. Lau's body dropping from sight replayed in his mind's eye. He couldn't hold his cousin's rage against her, but her absolute coldness in that act, the deliberate killing of Lau, made him cold too, in a different way. He was in no doubt the young man deserved it, and he would learn the full story, but it didn't make the murder any less permanent. And, if he were honest with himself, after seeing the man's eyes just before, that flash of a knife disappearing, he felt a certain satisfaction at Lau's death too. He looked back to Zi Yi as she descended to their cabin, and smiled. He loved his cousin, and if he took some pleasure in her strength and conviction, so be it. He was, after all, an imperfect man.

6

They tried to disguise Zi Yi as a young man, to avoid suspicion at her return and Lau's disappearance, but it was not convincing. The people on board had seen all three of them so frequently, for so long, the ruse would never stick. So she stayed mostly below decks, out of sight, out of mind, only rising for fresh air at night, disguised as Lau. They told anyone who asked that Lau was sick, and he chose to stay in the cabin. Fear of illness in the close quarters of a ship was enough to stop people asking any further questions, happy the young man had isolated himself.

Their first sight of Australia came a few days after her return, a distant view of Sydney Harbour. As they'd been told, Chinese weren't allowed to enter the country without a licence, nor even allowed off the ship to sightsee. It was the same at Port Melbourne later. Zi Yi regularly consulted her *luopan* and could only confirm that Bak Ma was still far away.

At last the steamer reached Port Adelaide in a sweltering heat. The cousins disembarked to be summarily processed and were told in no uncertain terms that the state of Victoria did not welcome *their kind*, and they should not go there. But the official's tone clearly implied that's exactly where he thought they would be heading, and he even surreptitiously pointed them in the right direction.

Once clear of the port's crowds, Zi Yi reached

into her bag, meaning to ask Crow Spirit to guide the way. She was dismayed to discover the tiny simulacrum was nothing more than a dried mess of pulp fragments, along with all her spirit paper, ruined by her gruelling journey through the waves. But her *luopan* now pointed strongly in a single direction, drawing her forward, so they would rely on that.

Their route was more often than not a dustbowl, and the tracks would frequently vanish, making the decision of which way forward one of luck as much as judgement, but Zi Yi's compass kept their destination true.

They struggled for water and food, the land a burning hellscape they had never anticipated. They took any containers they could find to collect and carry water, more than once looting the bodies of travellers less hardy than themselves.

"This place," Zi Yi said one day as they trudged under an incandescent sun. "I wonder why people think it's worth inhabiting."

"You remember those dark-skinned people we passed two days ago?" Yong Fa said. "We couldn't communicate and they eyed us with deep suspicion, but they looked healthy, no?"

Zi Yi nodded. "They did."

Yong Fa smiled. "I think perhaps it's not the land that is so inhospitable, moreso we are unsuited to it. If we knew the ways of those people, perhaps this place would be entirely more bearable."

"Indeed, cousin. Well, let's hope we can survive long enough to fulfill our purpose here and then leave for home. I would rather that."

Yong Fa laughed, the sound a scrape in his dry throat. "Me too."

Zi Yi found a scrap of notepad along the way that, while not spirit paper for a simulacrum, was good enough for spells. She wrote one for luck and protection, burned it, sprinkled the ashes into a cupful of their precious water and drank it down. "It will aid us," she promised.

Two days later they crossed the border into Victoria under cover of night, tipped off by a young man they had met that morning, who had learned the secret way in a letter from his uncle. Zi Yi smiled and wrote another spell, burned it, and drank that one down. "Better to be safe," she said. "The last one seems to have been used this night."

But the second spell was perhaps not so potent as the first. A day after entering the state of Victoria, they camped with a crew of rough and ready Europeans. They had met the four men on the trail that afternoon and had been initially cautious. But the group seemed friendly enough and between them, with broken English, they learned they were heading in a similar direction.

"The way it is danger," said their leader, Carlos. "Together, yes?"

So they decided to team up. The four men gave Yong Fa and Zi Yi some of their rations, cured meats and dried fruit. In return, the cousins shared some of their water. As night fell, they set up a camp together, building a fire in a scraped out bowl of red sand. Two of the men went off, carrying rifles. They returned sometime later, dragging the carcass of a strange animal. It's body was furred and grey-brown, thick set and strong, with short, stumpy legs and a broad head. Like a giant, muscular rat, Yong Fa mused as the men skinned and butchered it. But the meat, while gamey, was plentiful and they all ate their fill of it, roasted over the open fire. Zi Yi used her *luopan* to track down a small spring of fresh water while the men hunted. It took a long time, but eventually all their containers and canteens were filled again.

As the fire burned low, they each found an area of level ground and settled down to sleep.

"Cousin," Zi Yi whispered in the darkness. "Something is amiss."

"In what way?" Yong Fa was sleepy from a good feed, but trusted his cousin's instincts.

"There are bat spirits here, unlike any I've known before, and I only understand a tiny amount of their chatter, but they are cautious. They do not like these men, so therefore I don't like them either."

"They've been nothing but kind to us."

Zi Yi drew a long breath. "Too kind, in a way. I think they're softening us. Do me a favour? Stay awake while I sleep a few hours, then wake me to watch so you can sleep?"

"If you think so."

Zi Yi's instincts did indeed prove wise, and it saved their lives. She fell into a restless slumber and Yong Fa watched her as he lay on his side, feigning sleep. Drowsy though he was, he remained awake. After only an hour or so, he heard whispered conversation in a language he didn't recognise, but the intent was clear enough. All four men were planning something. He listened as they rose and moved almost silently in different directions. Had he been asleep, they would certainly have caught him by surprise. Instead, he was ready for them.

He waited until one had snuck almost to him, then pressed one hand to the dirt and swept his legs around. His shin connected with the man's ankles and took him clean off his feet. Yong Fa shouted Zi Yi's name as he surged up and leaped across her sleeping form, one leg pumping out in a kick to another man's chest as he stood over her. That man had a thick, silvered branch raised high, ready to beat her brains out.

Yong Fa's foot connected with his ribs and drove the wind from him. As Zi Yi scrambled up, Yong Fa hammered three quick, hard punches in and the attacker was unconscious. The man he had knocked off his feet rose again and the three remaining Europeans advanced in a semi-circle, faces angry, muttering in their guttural tongue.

"Stay behind me," Yong Fa said to his cousin. "This should not take long." He hoped he wasn't being over-confident.

Two of the men held branches of wood like the one he had just knocked out, the third was empty handed. But that one glanced to one side where the rifles lay, which decided Yong Fa on the order of his attack. He jumped to one side, spinning to crack a heel into that man's jaw. Taken completely by surprise, still looking at the rifles, the man's eyes glazed and he dropped. Yong Fa ducked and grabbed a long branch from the lowering fire. One end remained untouched by flame, the other a glowing red ember. Wielding it like a *jian*, the straight sword he'd always favoured while training at Shaolin, he advanced on the remaining two men. They looked at each other, then back to him, uncertain. That caution would end them. They advanced, branches held out before themselves.

Yong Fa used his weapon with skill, stepping in to meet them, batting each of their branches aside with quick, sweeping strikes of his burning brand. He lunged, struck one across the face, the man screaming and staggering back as the meat of his cheek sizzled, and Yong Fa turned to kick the other. That one tried valiantly to hit Yong Fa with his branch, but Yong Fa's brand circled around again, intercepted the blow and his foot cracked up under the man's chin. He dropped.

The last man standing, one hand pressed to his burned cheek, stared for a moment, then ran screaming into the night.

"Neatly done, cousin," Zi Yi said, as the three Yong Fa had felled moaned in the dark. "Let's grab our things, and perhaps some of theirs, and get away before they recover their senses."

"A good plan," Yong Fa agreed.

They collected all their own water and supplies, plus all they could carry from the men who would have robbed and no doubt killed them, and set off through the darkness. Once they had put an hour or more between themselves and the camp, Zi Yi said, "Let's rest here. I've had some sleep, it's your turn while I watch."

Yong Fa agreed, fatigue weighing heavy on him. In the lee of some rounded orange rocks, they settled down. It seemed he had only been asleep for moments when Zi Yi roused him again into a pink and grey dawn. Rising, gathering their things, they set off once more. Bak Ma had a lot to answer for, Yong Fa thought, as the heat of the day began to build again.

7

The country was criss-crossed with innumerable tracks of carts and drays that carved through dust and sand. Then the cousins crossed a swamp, then a rocky place, passed over creeks wet and dry, then a series of hills, only to venture finally into wide, endless plains. They passed broken wagons, abandoned, and many stark, white bones, both human and equine. Finding enough food was a constant trial and everything was so expensive when they did encounter people with whom to trade that they soon ran low on funds.

In camps here and there, they were pleased to find their own people, and were able to earn more with Zi Yi selling divinations, and Yong Fa begging alms, only to spend it almost immediately on over-priced sustenance.

Things become a little easier when a digger they befriended showed them how to eat better off the land. He taught them the secrets of damper and roasted cockatoo, and possum cooked on skewers, as well as tricks to catch those creatures, and others. He introduced them to unappetising bush fruits and grubs that would keep a person alive, after a fashion. He taught them useful English phrases that might help them survive. It was pleasant, Yong Fa mentioned, to meet someone genuinely friendly and helpful. The man was grateful for their company, it seemed, and repaid them with kindness. Zi Yi used a spell of good fortune on him when they parted ways and Yong Fa hoped it would pay off for him.

One afternoon as they rested under a tree, a strange spirit calling itself Kangaroo, approached. It was, it said, curious about Zi Yi's power, and offered to travel with them for a time, to warn of impending dangers, if she would allow it to study her. As a result they were able to hide and let bushrangers pass by, or take a different route to avoid ambushes. Zi Yi was grateful, unable to bear the thought of losing her treasured *luopan* to such attacks. Since Lau's assault she had taken to keeping it tucked deep inside her clothing, though she was uncertain how safe even that was. But pleased as she was with Kangaroo's protection, still she wondered how she would ever repay her debt to the kindly Spirit. However, the creature was benign and demanded nothing. When Zi Yi burned gum leaves as an offering in place of incense, Kangaroo seemed content with that. Other travellers weren't so lucky and the cousins regularly happened across a skeleton tied to a tree, a victim of bushrangers, left for the ants and eagles. This was a brutal, harsh land, with many brutal, harsh people in it. But also kind people, Yong Fa was quick to point out.

As they neared Ballarat they began to pass more established settlements. They saw sandstone buildings, shops and homes and farms. It was a blessed relief after the trials of the open country. They encountered coaches, travelling up from Melbourne, and enjoyed the glimpses of something close to civilisation, but they never lingered long, constantly pressing towards their goal. Kangaroo Spirit left them when the roads became busier, the land more populated.

The journey had squeezed out the last of any softness that remained in either cousin, and they arrived in Ballarat hardened and fuelled by a burning anger at all they'd been forced to endure and witness.

Ballarat was built on wide dirt streets criss-crossing undulating hills. Buildings of stone and weatherboard turned a brisk trade, their wide awnings providing welcome shade on the footpaths. The evidence of wealth was a stark contrast to the paucity of their journey. People were well-dressed, children and dogs ran and played everywhere, carts and horses busied the roads.

Agriculture was well established and evidence of industry, blacksmiths and foundries, was rife. Ballarat was a far bigger and more populated place than the cousins had anticipated. They walked along the main road, mouths agape.

"Where do we even begin?" Yong Fa asked.

"We should ask around," Zi Yi said. "The *luopan* indicated Bak Ma is that way, but still some distance off, I think. We could simply follow it, but some information first would be useful."

"These people don't seem very welcoming," Yong Fa observed.

They scanned the openly hostile white faces, tried to smile and show themselves to be no threat. Words and phrases were barked in their direction, but too quickly for them to catch, with a vocabulary they couldn't hope to follow. None of it seemed particularly friendly.

"We need to find some of our own people," Yong Fa said.

They turned away from the busy town centre and headed towards less populated places. Eventually they spotted a couple of Asian faces and greeted them warmly. "Where should we go to find welcome and rest?" Zi Yi asked them.

One man with a heavy Shanghai accent replied, "Nowhere in this country!" But he pointed towards the outskirts of town where the Chinese had established a community, including food vendors and boarding houses. The cousins thanked him and set off.

As the scowling, sharp faces gave way to more friendly visages, the cousins began to relax. Passing one group of Chinese arguing about whether the area's gold rush had run its course, they slowed to listen. "Mining is a fool's game now," one man said, and spat into the road.

"Better to turn our efforts to other pursuits before we're left with nothing but the clothes on our backs," agreed another.

Zi Yi gripped Yong Fa's arm tightly when a very skinny man said, "Not everywhere is dried up. That Bak Ma's mine is turning out gold like it was as plentiful as horse dung!"

"That is not a natural place and Bak Ma is not a natural man," said another, making a sign to ward off evil. "I would sooner starve than work for him."

"You may soon get that chance," said the first.

The cousins moved away and Zi Yi said, "The bastard is clearly making good use of our village's icon." Her face was pinched with rage.

"But we're getting close, so we can soon make it right," Yong Fa replied. He saw a *won-ton* seller on the street and smiled. "Look! Do we have enough money for a feed?"

Zi Yi nodded, her mood lightening at the sight of a familiar meal. She dug inside her *cheongsam*. "We'll be fed and housed for a couple more days before we need your antics again."

"My antics?"

Zi Yi grinned, puffed herself up in a mockery of Yong Fa's muscles. "Spare some alms for the love of the Buddha?" she said in a surprisingly accurate impression of his voice.

Yong Fa's mouth fell open in outrage and he was about to protest when a voice behind them said, "So you made it. We thought you'd died on the way."

"We hoped so, at least," said another.

They turned to face three men, each holding a pistol. Yong Fa's blood stilled. He hated guns with a passion. There was no honour, no skill. Any damn fool could pull a trigger.

"Crimson Cloud," Zi Yi said, voice dripping with disdain.

The man in the middle bowed, showing an ugly white scar across the top of his head that split his short, black hair in two.

"Bak Ma's divinations have foretold your arrival. We'd be happy to kill you where you stand, but the boss insists on seeing you." Scarhead gestured with the weapon towards a stage coach with its windows barred and padlocks on the doors, waiting to be secured.

8

The journey was rough and rattled their teeth for nearly an hour. It was stinking hot and close in the prison coach and they were offered neither food nor water. Their satchels had been taken from them, but they had not been searched. Zi Yi fussed over the lump of her *luopan* showing through her belt, though it was barely visible.

"I've retained it this far," she muttered. "I won't lose it now."

Yong Fa frowned, worried what might happen to Zi Yi if the thing was taken from her. He chose not to mention it further, but wished she was not so attached to that one material item, powerful though it was. Apart from anything else, it became something that could be used against her.

Peering through the bars, they watched the scrub give way to a small sea of white tents in a shallow valley. Beyond the tents was a huge, sprawling structure surrounded by a rough wooden paling fence. Three connected weatherboard buildings, two stories high, lined one side, with a wide brick chimney standing tall next to them, belching dark smoke into the massive blue sky. Beside the chimney a construction almost as high, built of scaffolded wooden beams, creaked as giant pulley wheels rotated at its top, busy ropes disappearing from it into the ground. On the opposite side were more buildings, brick and weatherboard stables, smaller latticed wood constructions. People swarmed everywhere.

"Bak Ma has certainly used the dragon to his advantage," Zi Yi said. She hissed between her teeth in disgust.

The coach drove between high gateposts into the main compound and pulled up outside the stables. It rocked as their three captors jumped down and hurried away, leaving Yong Fa and Zi Yi to swelter. Scarhead returned minutes later, his face split in a grin. "Bak Ma is very pleased to know you're here."

He made his gun obvious as he opened the door and gestured for them to climb out. As they emerged, two other men arrived to pat down the cousins. Yong Fa tensed, worried that Zi Yi was about to have her *luopan* discovered and to what that might drive her. As her searcher's hands moved towards her middle, she twisted slightly and snapped, "Have some respect with where you place your hands!"

The man grunted. "Stand still!" He continued to search, but Zi Yi's movement had caused him to skip the precious compass.

"He has nothing," Yong Fa's searcher said.

The other pulled Zi Yi's small purse from the top of her *cheongsam* and tossed it to Scarhead. "This is all she has."

"You would even rob our meagre coin?" Zi Yi asked.

"The dead have no need of money," Scarhead replied, and pocketed her purse. "Throw them in. Opposite ends so they can't talk."

The stables smelled strongly of straw and manure, horses whickered and snorted. Some of the stalls, Yong Fa realised, were cells, with floor to ceiling doors of iron bars. As he was pushed towards one end and Zi Yi to the other, they exchanged a knowing look. This would not end here.

"**My divinations were** right after all."

Yong Fa turned from investigating the back wall of his cell. "Zi Yi said you were nothing but a fraud," he said.

"Is that so?" Bak Ma replied. He moved closer to the bars of the door, resplendent in rich silks over a corpulent body, and dripping with gold jewellery. His braided hair glistened with expensive oils while his shaven pate gleamed. "I may not have her skills, but I'm no charlatan. No matter, though, for you'll both soon be dead. You don't cross Crimson Cloud and live."

"Earned your place now, then?" Yong Fa asked.

"I'm a rich and respected man."

"Only because of our Jade Dragon!"

Bak Ma laughed, his belly wobbling. "Strength belongs to he who takes it. An icon of such power was not meant to languish in a backwater village. That is an insult to its potency." The man dragged a silk kerchief over his brow. His nails were long.

"I don't care for this country, the heat, the flies, venomous creatures everywhere, but another year at most and I will return home, with untold wealth and respect, and with the Jade Dragon. Soon enough I'll be in control of Crimson Cloud. My influence will reach new heights, while your bones lie in an unmarked grave in this accursed red dirt."

"Don't be so sure."

"Your determination in making it this far is admirable, and I confess I am impressed, but it is over for you now."

"So why not just have your men shoot us?" Yong Fa asked, trembling at his audacity. "What are you waiting for?"

Bak Ma grinned. "Even I cannot yet control time. Government inspectors are due soon, to check our licences, so I must endure this bureaucratic annoyance. You are an inconvenience arriving today. But I had to see you, as you'd come this far. And now I have. Never fear, when the inspectors gone, I shall take my time with you *both*." He looked meaningfully to where Zi Yi was incarcerated, then back to Yong Fa with an evil grin.

Yong Fa bristled, his anger burning. Before he could say anything more, Bak Ma walked away.

Yong Fa could tell the thief had stopped at Zi Yi's cell at the other end of the long stables, and though he couldn't make out their conversation, he heard his cousin's outraged tone. He returned his attention to the brick wall at the back of his cell.

He focussed his rage and balled his fist. Gathering his *qi* into the strike, he punched one brick. It cracked through the middle and the mortar around it crumbled a little, fine dust raining down. Yong Fa drew breath again, and punched once more. Slowly, the wall of his prison began to respond to his will.

Far too slowly, but he would not give up.

9

Zi Yi swore she would kill herself before she allowed Bak Ma to make good on his lewd promises. But better to escape and destroy him instead. She had little time and would not squander it. She sat on the floor of packed earth, closed her eyes, and calmed her mind. Meditation allowed her consciousness to drift out into the world, seeking an ally.

"You've journeyed far," said a voice both familiar and strange.

Her astral self found it in the branches of a spreading eucalypt. She inclined her head. "As have you."

Crow Spirit bobbed and cawed, a sound quite unlike the crows she was used to. "Wherever there are my kind, so am I," he said. "But you travel the mundane way. Quite impressive."

"We can do anything, given enough time and will," Zi Yi said.

"The rabbit was well-received by Fox Spirit," Crow said. He seemed somehow contrite.

Zi Yi laughed. That seemed like another life, nearly a year and half a world away. "You're welcome."

"I'm sorry we were parted before my debt was fully repaid."

Crow Spirit *was* contrite. Zi Yi had quite happily thought the debt fulfilled, but the spirit obviously didn't. She remembered the words of its promise: *I'll stay with you until the man you seek is found.* "I've seen many crows in this land," she said. "Why wait until now to show yourself?"

"You did not call on me, and I thought you angry. I feared what retribution you might wreak. I saw Kangaroo Spirit offer you protection, so I remained silent. But I believe now you need assistance when she can't help. I would make peace with you."

"I do need help, yes."

"And if I provide it, our debt will be settled?"

Zi Yi smiled. "Get me out of this cell, and quickly, and we will most certainly be even."

Crow Spirit bobbed his head and flapped away.

Zi Yi dropped back into her physical body and ran to the door of the cell. She craned her neck to see out into the compound.

A crow swooped down from a tall tree and glided over to the tin roof of a nearby shed. It hopped lightly to the edge and looked over. Reclining in a battered, sun-bleached wooden chair was Scarhead, asleep. On a crooked nail on the wall behind him hung a ring of keys.

Crow Spirit launched himself from the roof and flapped under the eaves. Zi Yi held her breath as Scarhead stirred and leapt to his feet, waving his arms to shoo the bird away. The crow flew up and out of sight. Scarhead frowned and returned to his seat, and closed his eyes.

What now? Zi Yi thought. Had Crow Spirit

given up so easily?

Movement caught her eye as the crow walked on silent feet in the building's shadow. It cocked its head and two more of its kind swooped in. One shot straight at Scarhead and pecked hard at his knee. Zi Yi laughed as the man leapt up with a cry and ran, swiping at the bird as the second dive-bombed him from above. He flailed and swore as several passing miners paused to watch. They hid their smiles, too scared, it seemed, to laugh openly.

Under cover of the mayhem, Crow Spirit grabbed the heavy ring of keys and flew off crooked and low, weighed down by its burden. When he was safely out of sight, the other two birds ceased their attack to return to the trees, leaving Scarhead to look around himself in confusion.

"What are you all gawping at?" he yelled. "Get back to work!"

As the gathered crowd scurried away, Scarhead returned to his seat, glaring up at the blue gums around the compound.

Camouflaged in the shadows of the stables, Crow Spirit dropped the keys just outside Zi Yi's cell door. She reached through, grabbed them and fumbled for the right one. On the third try, the lock clicked and her door swung open.

"Our debt is cleared?" Crow Spirit asked.

"Yes," she said. "And thank you."

"Perhaps one day we can do each other favours again?"

Zi Yi crouched and scratched the bird's neck. "Perhaps we can."

The crow flapped off and she hurried along to Yong Fa's cell, sticking to the shadows. Yong Fa's knuckles bled. The bricks in front of him were cracked and tiny pinpricks of light showed through. The wall looked as if it were about to collapse.

"Don't make any more noise, you fool!" Zi Yi said. "Brute force is not always the answer." She found the right key and let him out. "Quickly, let's go."

"Cousin, you are a wonder," Yong Fa said with a smile.

The noise of a coach arriving at the compound gates stilled them. Shiny beneath its cover of road dust, it was considerably better than the one they'd travelled in. Scarhead ran to open the nearest door and two white men in expensive-looking suits emerged.

"Perfect timing," Yong Fa said with a grin. "Just the distraction we need. Where to now?"

Zi Yi patted the small bulge of the *luopan*. "Hopefully this will tell us." She pulled it free and turned its filigree wheels. "This is better for people and places, but perhaps this close..?" She put her will into it, *Show me the Jade Dragon*. The sensation of drag was downwards, right beneath her feet. She adjusted dials and used her magic again before nodding to the giant rope and pulley system used to lower men into the mine in a wooden cage elevator. "It's down there," she said.

Checking that no one looked their way, they

scurried for the shadows under the tall chimney and pulley housing. One man stood guard and two more leaned against a wheel used to raise and lower the cage.

"I can take care of them," Yong Fa said. "But who will operate the machine?"

"We can lower it ourselves then climb down the ropes?" Zi Yi suggested.

"Good plan," Yong Fa said. "Won't be a moment."

He stepped from their hiding place and approached the men with a broad smile and palms raised. "Brothers, would you care to hear about the peace that regular meditation can bring to the workplace?"

"Who in all the hells are you?" cried the guard.

Yong Fa kept smiling and didn't slow until he was directly in front of the man. Then his hands flashed, one, two, three quick, perfectly targeted strikes. The guard stiffened, eyes wide, and he tipped over like a plank of wood. Yong Fa stepped over him even as he fell and rushed the two gaping lift operators. Their hands began to rise in self-defence, but Yong Fa's steps were like dancing as he moved gracefully between them, a strike here, a kick there, and they fell limply to the red earth.

Grabbing a coil of rope that lay nearby, the monk wound it around and around, trussing the three men tightly together. As they began to stir and moan, he struck hard and fast with extended index and middle fingers, finding the precise pressure points to ensure a long, deep sleep. He dragged the heavy bundle into the gloom under a scored wooden bench and turned to Zi Yi. The smile hadn't left his face the whole time. "Shall we?"

Zi Yi bowed and between them they heaved against the large wooden wheel that operated the chains and ropes of the rack and pulley system high above, and the wooden cage disappeared down into the mine. It took several minutes of hard work and sweat, all the time frantic that someone would appear and find them, but it seemed the camp was pre-occupied with the officials' visit. Finally they felt the bump that told them the lift had hit the bottom.

Yong Fa jumped into the shaft and caught the rope. He began to descend hand under hand, his feet wrapped below him to control his speed. Zi Yi let him get a few yards ahead before taking a deep breath and climbing in far more carefully than her cousin had.

Immediately the air became cool, a thankful relief from the sweltering day above. They passed several dark horizontal shafts supported by mortised wooden beams, but Zi Yi would shake her head each time Yong Fa looked up. "Further down."

Faint lantern light glowed from side tunnels below, the shaft seemingly endless.

Zi Yi called, "My grip is failing. I need to rest."

Yong Fa shook his head. "We don't have time. Slide down and wrap your legs around my waist."

"You can't take my weight!"

He looked up and raised an eyebrow. "If there's one thing I'm good for, it's this. I have strength enough for us both. When we're safe on solid ground, you concentrate on finding the right course. Together we're stronger in every way than if we try to do it all alone."

Reluctantly Zi Yi slid down and wrapped herself around him like a monkey to its mother. Yong Fa felt her heart hammering through her chest and she shook, her breath hard against his neck.

He continued down and soon they began to pass brighter tunnels, the ringing of hammers and scrape of shovels drifting to their ears. Occasionally they spotted people moving. Then the inhabited passages ended and the shaft dropped into deeper shadow.

"One level further, I can feel it," Zi Yi said. "But the lift is blocking the tunnel we need!"

Distant shouting erupted from above.

They glanced up, but there was only a tiny square of bright light far overhead. The rope began to move.

"They're bringing up the cage!" Zi Yi said.

Not far below, the elevator shuddered and began to rise. Yong Fa redoubled his speed, his palms burning from the friction as he tried to descend faster than the pulley system could raise him, but for every two feet he climbed down, they were carried one back up.

"Hold tight!" he shouted, and released his grip.

Zi Yi yelped in surprise as they dropped

like stones. They hit the roof of the rising lift with a jarring impact that made the wooden roof creak and threaten to crack. Yong Fa flexed his legs to absorb the landing and said, "Into the tunnel!"

They dropped and rolled. With less than two feet to spare they tumbled through the gap between the cage and the roof of the nearest passageway and dropped with heavy breaths to the floor.

They lay still, breathing hard, as the elevator rattled away above them. "Are you okay?" Yong Fa asked eventually.

Zi Yi stood unsteadily and patted herself down. "I think so. But we're one level too high."

They returned to the opening and clambered over the edge to use the beams that reinforced the shaft like a giant ladder, and then dropped the last few feet to the very bottom of the mine. Zi Yi consulted her *luopan* in the last of the lambent light from above. "This way."

"It's very quiet. There's not much activity here," Yong Fa observed.

"At least there's no one to challenge us," Zi Yi said. "Is there?"

"We only have as long as it takes that lift to reach the surface and come back again to find out."

"And then what?"

"We'll deal with that when we get to it."

They stepped into the tunnel and further darkness until Zi Yi whispered, "I can't see anything."

"Keep one hand on the wall and tread

carefully."

They moved cautiously and soon a soft glow began to fill the space, like a hundred fireflies lived somewhere far ahead. The light was weak but it turned the pitch black into a kind of twilight, and they could at least see the floor.

"That's a bit of luck," Yong Fa said.

"Is it?" Zi Yi said tightly. "There's something here, I feel it. And it may not be benevolent."

"Only one way to find out." Yong Fa jogged off along the cold tunnel.

When the passageway opened out into a cavern, the source of the luminescence became plain. In a small indentation in the rock wall, glowing brightly, sat the Jade Dragon. Its green, shimmering light rippled along the walls like water.

"Aha!" Yong Fa exclaimed.

"Wait!" Zi Yi looked around with a frown. "This is too easy."

"Too easy? Do you remember everything we went through to get here?"

"Yes! And after all that it's just sitting there, ripe for the plucking? No, Bak Ma is more cautious than that. I think perhaps this is exactly why there's a dark and empty tunnel behind us. It's been dug for this one purpose."

She moved slowly forward and, as she got to within a few feet of the dragon, a low buzzing rose. She threw herself backwards as dozens of tiny black bolts shot from hidden niches to pepper the ground where she had been standing. She threw Yong Fa an *I-told-you-so* look. He shrugged, repentant.

"And look there," she said. "That slab in front of the dragon looks loose. Another trap. And maybe there are more. I need time to explore."

Rattles and shouts drifted to them along the tunnel. "I don't think there's much time left, cousin," Yong Fa said. "But I'll give you all I can." Without waiting for a reply, he ran back the way they had come.

His only advantage was surprise and he kept low and close to the wall. He reached the lift shaft just as the cage was settling into place. A dozen men were crammed inside, all brandishing large machetes. As they burst out, Yong Fa broke from the shadows and struck, left and right. There were a couple of shovels against one wall and he grabbed one, wielding it first like a staff, then like a hoe, then chopped with it like a strange sword.

He deflected attacks, the machetes clanging starkly against the metal like bells ringing, then the duller peal of the shovel cracking heads. He kicked out the knee of one man and turned to slam a fist into the side of another's head. He whirled his makeshift weapon and took out two more. The tightness of the tunnel was to his advantage, preventing the mob from surrounding him, and he laughed as he danced and moved, punched and kicked, blocked and swung, in his element against foes who could only attack one or two at a time and stood no chance in the face of his skills. Zi Yi would have plenty of time before another contingent could be sent down.

As the last thug fell, a loud *click* echoed in the sudden quiet. Bak Ma stepped from the shadows at the back of the cage with a pistol pointed at Yong Fa's head. "Most impressive," the fat man said. "But your old-fashioned techniques are no match for modern industry." He gestured with the barrel. "Let's go and find your cousin, shall we?"

Yong Fa ground his teeth. How he hated guns.

10

The sounds of fighting soon began to echo back, but Zi Yi ignored them and gathered a handful of the fallen bolts that had fired from the wall. Careful not to get too close, she threw them towards the Jade Dragon and triggered another volley to erupt into the cave. Did Bak Ma have a limitless supply somehow embedded there? Given the fortune he had amassed, it seemed possible he could afford endless defences.

Again she gathered a handful of bolts and threw them forward, and another hail peppered the ground. But fewer this time. Perhaps she could exhaust the trap. Three further handfuls and no more tiny arrows were forthcoming. Wincing against the possibility of error, Zi Yi crept forward.

The glow of the dragon intensified, and the sensation of presence grew stronger as she neared it. She needed time to concentrate, to investigate the spirit realms, but time was exactly what she didn't have. The distant sounds of fighting stilled and silence fell around her.

Refusing to think what that might mean, she approached the strange slab in the floor. Though the bay was large enough to accommodate a couple of people, the smooth-cut slab covered the ground completely. There wasn't any way to approach the dragon without stepping on the great tile. She took a handful of the spent quarrels from the floor and cautiously tossed them in. A rumbling shook the cave and Zi Yi cried out as a metal grill slammed down from above, raking fire across her back as she leapt forward, only just managing to avoid being impaled by it. The back of her *cheongsam* hung in tatters and her scored flesh bled and burned. But though she was still alive, she found herself trapped in a floor to ceiling cage with the dragon.

Wicked laughter bounced off the walls and she spun around to see Bak Ma holding a gun to Yong Fa's head.

"Did you really think you could outsmart me?"

"You'll pay for what you've done," Yong Fa said. "One way or another, you'll pay."

Bak Ma jabbed him with the weapon. "Will I? I think not. But you two will never see daylight again."

Biting down her rage, Zi Yi ignored Bak Ma's narcissistic ranting and closed her eyes. She had no choice now but to search desperately for help from elsewhere and that strange drifting presence was her only hope. Ignoring Bak Ma's chatter, she sat down, opened her mind to the spirits and called out. "I need assistance! Please, is anyone there? I would make any bargain you desire. I need assistance!"

"And perhaps I can give it." The voice, regal and powerful, rang with the wisdom of ages.

"Who are you?" Zi Yi asked, shocked by the presence. "Where are you?"

"Behind you."

Zi Yi turned her astral eye to the dragon she had crossed half the world to find. With her otherworldly vision, she saw something swirling within the jade carving, twisting and pressing. "Who are you?" she asked again.

"I am Loong Jin Tien, and I have been trapped for a long time. Your ancestor, Yao Gailing, used powerful magic to crack open my mountain and trick me into entering this jade prison."

"No, no! Yao Gailing is the hero of our village! The dragon *helped* him to found our home and gave him the jade for this carving."

"That's what he would have you believe. But I was pressed into service against my will. My presence brings fortune to everyone but me."

Zi Yi was horrified. "Why haven't you called out before?"

"Yao's enchantment was so strong that I could only converse with one who addressed me directly, and no one with power has spoken to this simple jade icon before. Even you have done so now only in despair." Reproach saturated its tone. "So often have looked upon me, so often I have silently begged you to converse with me, but you never saw through Yao's enchantment. You never saw anything more than jade. Until now."

"Then you have been done a great wrong and we owe you an enormous debt," Zi Yi said. "And I would repay it."

"And I will assist you if you do."

"My only real decision," Bak Ma was saying, "is whether to kill you while your sweet cousin watches, then have my way with her, or have my way with her while *you* watch, then kill you both."

Yong Fa ground his teeth. He only needed a moment and a tiny amount of space in which to manoeuvre, but Bak Ma seemed to sense that and gave him no quarter, the gun barrel pressed hard against his skull. Zi Yi sat in a trance, eyes closed. She couldn't have simply given up, but what could she do behind bars, deep underground?

Then, suddenly, his cousin stood. Yong Fa tensed, ready for any opportunity to move, but Bak Ma's gun didn't waver.

Zi Yi turned and grabbed the Jade Dragon from its small pedestal and raised it high above her head.

"What are you doing?" Bak Ma screamed, but the only answer she gave was to dash the priceless icon hard against the stone tile embedded in the floor.

Bak Ma staggered in shock and Yong Fa took his chance. He ducked and thrust one elbow back even as the trigger was pulled. The sound of the shot deafened him and a score of pain seared against the side of his head. But it was only a graze and he had Bak Ma's wrist in his grip and he twisted it.

The bones broke, and the gun fell from Bak Ma's fingers as he yelped in pain. The Jade Dragon hit the ground and shattered into a thousand pieces. Yong Fa sent Bak Ma staggering with a powerful palm to the sternum as light and smoke swirled and filled the cave.

A dragon twisted into being and pressed up against the bars, its sinuous form bright green on top with cream scales along the length of its belly. Long, scarlet whiskers and beard whipped in the wind of its appearance, the golden claws of its five-fingered hands and feet scored grooves in the rock. It ducked its mighty head and the metal bars crumpled before it like paper and the dragon continued to grow.

As Bak Ma tried to stagger to his feet and flee, the dragon grabbed him in its powerful jaws. Ignoring his high shrieks of panic, the mighty beast gently gathered Yong Fa and Zi Yi, each in one hot, clawed hand, and shot off along the tunnel. Holding them protectively to its hard scales, it flew. It crashed through the lift and straight up the mineshaft at eye-watering speed to burst out into blinding sunlight. The tower and pulley smashed into pieces and collapsed into the shaft as the dragon flew high into the blistering blue sky. The mine and camp withered to a pinprick in the distance below.

Loong Jin Tien writhed in the air as if

luxuriating in cool water.

"This cannot be!" Bak Ma screamed, trying to force the jaws apart.

The dragon tossed him upwards. "Oh, yes it can," it boomed. "And you have used me for your own selfish ends for long enough!"

As Bak Ma tumbled back down, the dragon snaked forward and snapped him from the air. Yong Fa and Zi Yi gasped as the lump of Bak Ma slid down Loong Jin Tien's throat.

Sweeping through the air with its eyes shut, the dragon said, "Oh, it is so good to be free!"

"If I had known, I would have released you sooner," Zi Yi said. "Anyone in our village would."

Loong Jin Tien held them up before his face. "Perhaps not everyone, but I believe you would have, little one. Your people's devotion to me was a salve of sorts, and I can't blame you for something of which you knew nothing. And Yao Gailing has long since passed beyond my vengeance. But I am free now."

The dragon flew over scrub and bush to land far from prying eyes. It set the cousins down.

"Our mission turned out to be more important than I ever realised," Zi Yi said. "I'm so happy we have given you your liberty again."

"And if there's anything else we can do please tell us," Yong Fa said. "We owe you our lives."

Loong Jin Tien rumbled soft laughter. "You've done enough. But remember something for me, human," he said to Zi Yi.

"Of course. Anything!"

"Whenever you see a carved icon, take a

moment to stop and speak with it. All the offerings of fruit and incense in the world are very nice, but they don't compare to freedom."

"I promise I will, great dragon."

The majestic head nodded, then looked up to the sky with longing. "I shall dance among the clouds for years before I rest again," Loong Jin Tien said. "But first, may I return you to Long-en?"

"Yes, please!" Yong Fa said. "While this land is fascinating, I will not miss it. But I do miss the valleys of home."

Loong Jin Tien lifted them onto his back. "Then hold tight." He launched again into the blue.

Zi Yi leaned forward. "Mighty dragon, might I ask you final favour?"

"Of course."

"There is an island I must find, a promise to Dolphin Spirit I need to keep." Zi Yi looked apologetically back at Yong Fa. "Will you tell my parents, cousin? Tell them not to worry and assure them I will return as soon as I am able."

"What makes you think you're going anywhere without me?" Yong Fa asked.

"The village needs to know what has occurred."

Yong Fa shook his head. "Do they really though? They have survived all the time we've been away, without the luck of their icon. Haven't they, Loong Jin Tien?"

"They have," the great dragon said. "My

incarceration brought them luck, but Long-en has long been a well-established, stable and happy place. They certainly don't need my presence any more than anywhere else does. And I might visit from time to time anyway. Perhaps I could let your family know you are safe and all is well. Shall I tell them you will return eventually and not to worry?"

Zi Yi laughed. "I can only imagine my father's reaction to you and to such news. But yes, would you really do that for us?"

"Certainly. Once I have dropped you where you need to be, I will let your family know. And I will be discreet so as not to set the village into a furore."

"So it's settled then," Yong Fa said. "Thank you, Loong Jin Tien."

"Are you certain?" Zi Yi asked, her hair whipping in the wind of their flight. "You'll accompany me?"

Yong Fa laughed. "Of course. You're not going to enjoy adventures and leave me to miss out. Besides, who knows what might happen without me to look out for you?"

Acknowledgements

I want to thank Lindy Cameron of Clan Destine Press for originally commissioning this yarn. The only reason this story exists is because she asked me for something for the *And Then..?* anthology and this is the result. I also want to thank my kung fu brother and fellow disciple, James Lui, who read the early draft of this story and made sure my Chinese names were correct and that I hadn't made any cultural faux pas. Any mistakes that have made it into the story are entirely my fault. Lastly, my heartfelt thanks to my Sifu, Grandmaster Chen Yong Fa. I used his name for one of the lead characters in this story, but that's not nearly enough to repay all he has given me. Thank you, Sifu.

ABOUT ALAN BAXTER

Alan Baxter is a multi-award-winning British-Australian author of horror, supernatural thrillers, and dark fantasy. He's also a martial arts expert, a whisky-soaked swear monkey, and dog lover. He creates dark, weird stories among dairy paddocks on the beautiful south coast of NSW, Australia. The author of over twenty books including novels, novellas, and several short story collections, you can find him online at www.alanbaxter.com.au Feel free to tell him what you think. About anything.